SUMMERHOUSE

A DK Ink Book

Published in Canada in 1999 by
Stoddart Kids,
a division of Stoddart Publishing Co. Limited
34 Lesmill Road
Toronto, Canada M3B 2T6
Tel (416) 445-3333 Fax (416) 445-5967
E-mail Customer.Service@ccmailgw.genpub.com

Distributed in Canada by
General Distribution Services
325 Humber College Blvd.
Toronto, Canada M9W 7C3
Tel (416) 213-1919 Fax (416) 213-1917
E-mail Customer.Service@ccmailgw.genpub.com

Published in the United States in 1999 by DK Ink, DK Publishing Inc., New York

Canadian Cataloguing in Publication Data
Anholt, Laurence
Summerhouse
ISBN 0-7737-3152-0
I. Russell, Lynne. II. Title.
PZ7.A54Su 1999 j823'.914 C98-932314-5

SUMMERHOUSE

LAURENCE ANHOLT • ILLUSTRATED BY LYNNE RUSSELL

Stoddart
Kids

For Sam
and Hannah White,
with love—L.A.

For Robert,
with all my love—L.R.

WHEN ELLA'S GRANDMA LAUGHED,
it started like a tiny tickle, deep
down inside.

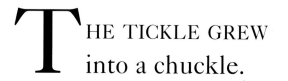

T HE TICKLE GREW
into a chuckle.

The chuckle grew
into a rumble.

The rumble grew
into a shake.

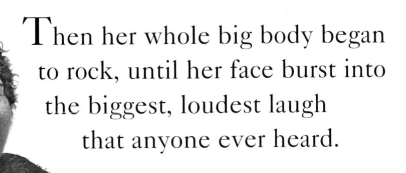

Then her whole big body began
to rock, until her face burst into
the biggest, loudest laugh
that anyone ever heard.

And soon everyone
had caught it—like
sneezes in winter.
And nobody could stop.
Not Ella's grandpa
or Ella's mom,
or even Ella's dad.

But Ella didn't laugh.
Ella was a serious girl.

Although Ella loved her grandma,
she just didn't get the joke.

ELLA'S GRANDMA AND GRANDPA had moved to this old house many years before Ella was even born. They had left their tiny island home and sailed to this big cold country so Grandpa could find a job.

And the first thing Grandpa had done
was to build a summerhouse for
Grandma at the end of the garden.
To remind her of the brightly colored
beach huts back home.

B<small>UT THAT WAS A LONG TIME AGO.</small> Now it was winter in this faraway town and Grandpa's hair was as white as the snow on the summerhouse roof.

Now they all sat inside and listened to Grandpa telling stories about their island home in the blue-green ocean.

But Ella stood by the window and looked at the thick, gray snow.

It gave her a strange feeling. Sort of bored. Sort of sad. Sort of winter inside.

ONE DAY, GRANDMA SAID, "Listen, Ella. You're too young to be so serious. You have to find some sunshine inside yourself—even when it's winter.

"That's why I'm so big," Grandma grinned, "because I have the *whole* sun inside me!"

Grandma hugged her close. "Here's something
for you, girl," she whispered, holding out a long
brass key. "The key to the summerhouse.
Now wrap up warm and run out to play."

T HERE WERE NO OTHER FOOTPRINTS
in the silent garden as Ella walked
across the snow. She looked back at her family,
laughing and laughing inside. She tried to find the
sunshine inside herself, but it just wasn't there.

Ella climbed the icy wooden steps to the summerhouse door and pushed the key in the lock. She turned the handle and shoved hard, but the door was frozen shut. So Ella kicked it hard.

THE DOOR SWUNG OPEN JUST A LITTLE. Just a tiny crack. A warm light was shining from inside.

Then the door burst open, and Ella fell right inside the summerhouse and tumbled onto the floor.

IT WAS WARM IN THERE
and the noise was loud.
Sort of surf sighing.
Sort of seabirds crying.
Sort of palm leaves rustling.

Then Ella smelled a strange smell.
Sort of wild flowers.
Sort of coconut oil.
Sort of salty sand.

Then Ella felt a strange feeling.
Sort of warm wind blowing.
Sort of sunshine on skin.
Sort of summertime.

SHE SAT UP. She looked around.
Her eyes popped wide.
Ella was sitting on top of a silvery beach,
high above a cool, clear blue-green sea
scattered with tiny islands. Behind her,
palm trees danced, butterflies floated,
and hummingbirds hovered around
huge rainbow flowers.

ELLA STOOD UP. She looked down at
her winter clothes and her big red boots.
And the smallest, tiniest smile crept across her face.

Ella pulled off her scarf and dropped it on the sand.

She pulled off her coat and kicked her big red boots high into the sky.

Ella tore off her socks and wiggled her toes in the hot, hot sand.

THEN SHE BEGAN TO RUN. Down the endless empty beach to the endless empty sea.

Sort of swimming.

Sort of floating.

Sort of diving.

Down, down,
deep as a dolphin,
then rushing and
bursting for air.

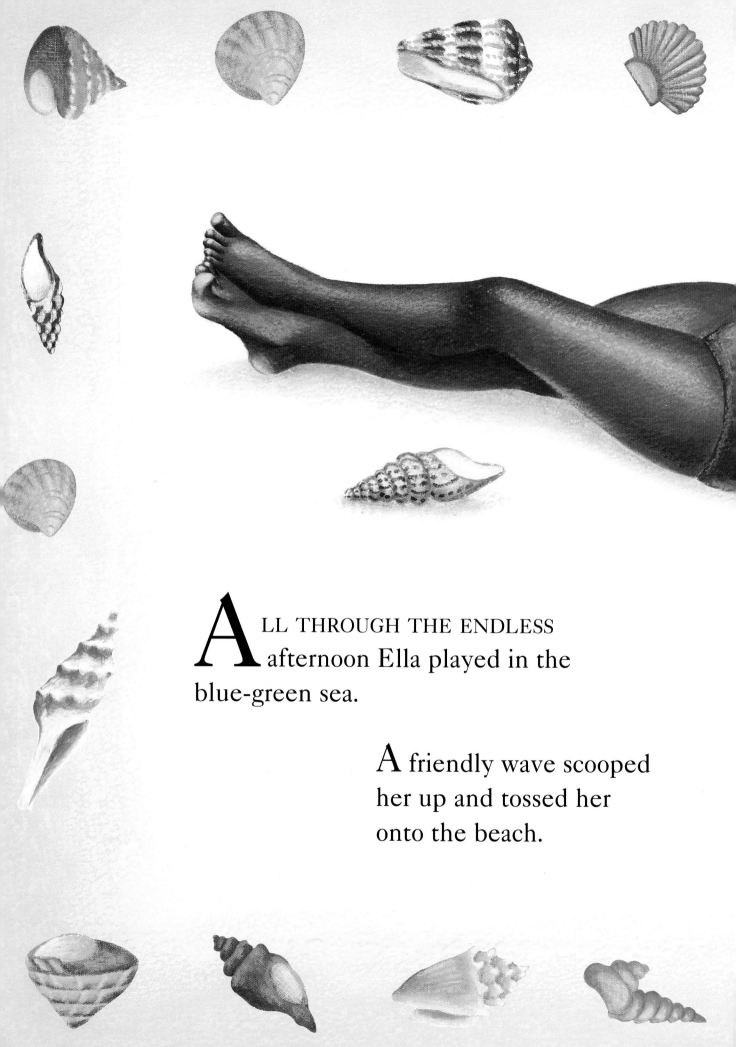

ALL THROUGH THE ENDLESS afternoon Ella played in the blue-green sea.

A friendly wave scooped her up and tossed her onto the beach.

A warm wind dried her skin
and powdered her with sand.

High above her head,
the sun shone down,
bright as Grandma's smile.

So ELLA DIDN'T MIND when it was time to go.
Now that she knew where the sunshine was,
she could come any time she pleased.
She ran back to the summerhouse
and pulled on her winter clothes.

Then Ella closed the summerhouse door,
locked it carefully with the brass key, and
hurried through the snowy garden
back to Grandma's house.

S HE CLIMBED WAY UP onto Grandma's lap and slipped the key into her hand. Ella had a feeling that Grandma knew about the summerhouse, too.

And when Grandma started tickling, Ella smiled. It was like sun breaking through clouds.

The tickle turned into a chuckle.

The chuckle turned into a rumble.

The rumble grew into a shake.

And Ella burst out laughing, the loudest laugh that anyone had ever heard. Until Grandma caught it, too—like sneezes in winter.

AT LAST ELLA YAWNED and curled
up small and fell fast asleep on
Grandma's lap. She felt a warm new
feeling somewhere deep, deep down.

Sort of summer in winter.
Sort of sunshine inside.
Sort of *happy*.